SQUARE
FISH

Henry Holt and Company

Tikki Tikki Tembo

retold by Arlene Mosel / illustrated by Blair Lent

Square Fish
An Imprint of Macmillan Publishers

ISBN-10: 0-312-36748-1
ISBN-13: 978-0-312-36748-0

Originally published in the United States by
Henry Holt and Company, LLC

First Square Fish Edition: June 2007

10 9 8 7 6 5 4

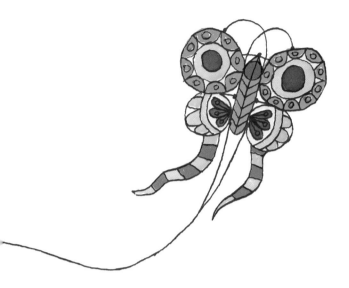

Once upon a time, a long, long time ago, it was the custom
of all the fathers and mothers in China to give their first and
honored sons great long names. But second sons were given
hardly any name at all.

In a small mountain village there lived a mother who had
two little sons. Her second son she called Chang, which
meant "little or nothing." But her first and honored son,
she called Tikki tikki tembo-no sa rembo-chari bari ruchi-
pip peri pembo, which meant "the most wonderful thing
in the whole wide world!"

Every morning the mother went to wash in a little stream near her home. The two boys always went chattering along with her. On the bank was an old well.

"Don't go near the well," warned the mother, "or you will surely fall in."

The boys did not always mind their mother and one day they were playing beside the well, and on the well when Chang fell in!

Tikki tikki tembo-no sa rembo-chari bari ruchi-pip peri pembo ran as fast as his little legs could carry him to his mother and said,

"Most Honorable Mother, Chang has fallen into the well!"

"The water roars, 'Little Blossom,' I can not hear you," said the mother.

Then Tikki tikki tembo-no sa rembo-chari bari ruchi-pip peri pembo raised his voice and cried,

"Oh, Most Honorable One, Chang has fallen into the well!"

"That troublesome boy," answered the mother. "Run and get the Old Man With The Ladder to fish him out."

Then Tikki tikki tembo-no sa rembo-chari bari ruchi-pip peri pembo ran as fast as his little legs could carry him to the Old Man With The Ladder and said,

"Old Man With The Ladder, Chang has fallen into the well. Will you come and fish him out?"

"So," said the Old Man With The Ladder, "Chang has fallen into the well."

And he ran as fast as his old legs could carry him. Step over step, step over step he went into the well, picked up little Chang, and step over step, step over step brought him out of the well.

He pumped the water out of him and pushed the air into him, and pumped the water out of him and pushed the air into him, and soon Chang was just as good as ever!

Now for several months the boys did not go near the well. But after the Festival of the Eighth Moon they ran to the well to eat their rice cakes.

They ate near the well, they played around the well, they walked on the well and Tikki tikki tembo-no sa rembo-chari bari ruchi-pip peri pembo fell into the well!

Chang ran as fast as his little legs could carry him to his mother and said,

"Oh, Most Honorable Mother, Tikki tikki tembo-no sa rembo-chari bari ruchi-pip peri pembo has fallen into the well!"

"The water roars, 'Little One,' I cannot hear you."

So little Chang took a deep breath.

"Oh, Mother, Most Honorable," he panted, "Tikki tikki tembo-no sa rembo-chari bari ruchi-pip peri pembo has fallen into the well!"

"Tiresome Child, what are you trying to say?" said his mother.

"Honorable Mother!
Chari bari
rembo
tikki tikki,"
he gasped,
"pip pip
has fallen into the well!"
"Unfortunate Son, surely the evil spirits have bewitched
your tongue. Speak your brother's name with reverence."

Poor little Chang was all out of breath from saying that great long name, and he didn't think he could say it one more time. But then he thought of his brother in the old well.

Chang bowed his little head clear to the sand, took a deep breath and slowly, very slowly said,

"Most Honorable Mother, Tikki tikki—tembo-no—sa rembo—chari bari—ruchi-pip—peri pembo is at the bottom of the well."

"Oh, not my first and honored son, heir of all I possess! Run quickly and tell the Old Man With The Ladder that your brother has fallen into the well."

So Chang ran as fast as his little legs would carry him to the Old Man With The Ladder. Under a tree the Old Man With The Ladder sat bowed and silent.

"Old Man, Old Man," shouted Chang. "Come right away! Tikki tikki tembo-no sa rembo-chari bari ruchi-pip peri pembo has fallen into the stone well!"

But there was no answer. Puzzled he waited. Then with his very last bit of breath he shouted,

"Old Man With The Ladder, Tikki tikki tembo-no sa rembo-chari bari ruchi-pip peri pembo is at the bottom of the well."

"Miserable child, you disturb my dream. I had floated into a purple mist and found my youth again. There were glittering gateways and jeweled blossoms. If I close my eyes perhaps I will again return."

Poor little Chang was frightened. How could he say that great long name again?

"Please, Old Man With The Ladder, please help my brother out of the cold well."

"So," said the Old Man With The Ladder, "your mother's 'Precious Pearl' has fallen into the well!"

The Old Man With The Ladder hurried as fast as his old legs could carry him. Step over step, step over step he went into the well, and step over step, step over step out of the well with the little boy in his arms. Then he pumped the water out of him and pushed the air into him, and pumped the water out of him and pushed the air into him.

But little Tikki tikki tembo-no sa rembo-chari bari ruchi-pip peri pembo had been in the water so long, all because of his great long name, that the moon rose many times before he was quite the same again.

And from that day to this the Chinese have always thought it wise to give all their children little, short names instead of great long names.